Best of
Psychological
TALES

TINY TOT PUBLICATIONS
INDIA

Best of

Psychological

TALES

© TINY TOT PUBLICATIONS 2009

This Edition:-2009

Written by:

Zakir Ali 'Rajneesh'

Edited by:

Shyam Dua

Published By:

TINY TOT PUBLICATIONS

A-164, Sector-63
Nodia-201301 (U.P.)
Ph.: 93101 67314, 93101 63582
Fax : 0120-4281696
Regd. Office: 235, Jagriti Enclave
Delhi-110 092 (INDIA)
Ph.: 2216 7314
e-mail : tinytotpub@hotmail.com
Website : www.tinytotpub.com

ISBN : 81-304-0151-7

Illustrated by

Bookmark

Although Sonu was always at fault, Anjum always blamed the teachers. Thus, he formed a negative impression against the teachers.

This was the reason that he protested when his parents were preparing Anjum for the admission. He thought that there was no freedom in the school. So he constantly refused to go to school.

His parents were worried to see his aversion to school. They allured him to find out the reason of his disliking to go to school so that they could find a solution. ...... After much efforts and persuasion they were able to prepare Anjum to go to school. They got him admitted in the nursery class.

It was the first day for Anjum in the school. He was thinking about his teacher's personality—dreadful face, sporting a stick in his hand and staring eyes behind the big spectacles.

He continued to think of the teacher's frightening staring eyes and the stick that he could use when something went wrong. Every moment was passing with great worry.

"Good morning madam!" The sharp sound echoed in the class. Anjum looked up. A lady teacher was standing in the class. She was just the opposite of the teacher in his imagination.

He saw that the teacher had a very pleasing appearance. She neither had spectacles on her eyes nor a stick in her hand. She wished good morning to the students, and sat on her chair. Her voice was very sweet. Anjum's horrible image of the teacher was shattered. He did not get up to say good morning to the teacher. But by the time he got up other students said, "Thank you miss," and sat down.

The teacher was already seated on her chair. She saw Anjum and smiled, "You are our new student, come to me." Anjum got up from his seat and moved towards the teacher hesitatingly. He stood before the teacher, looked up on her face and said, "Will you beat

me?" "Who told you that I beat!" saying so she laughed. She further added, "You are a very good boy, very sweet really." Then she picked him up and held him in her lap. Caressing his hair she asked him, "What is your good name?" "Anjum", said he with a smile.

"Oh, very good name! Do you know the meaning of your name?"

He replied in negative. The teacher said, "It means a star—the little shining and twinkling star in the sky. They are very lovely .Likewise you are also the star of your parents."

"You are also very nice, just like my Mom," said Anjum to the teacher. He was no longer scared.

The teacher said, " You are very sweet. Do you know the alphabets?"

Anjum said, "I know all from A to Z."

"All right, Go to your seat. I am just going to ask you

the alphabet." The teacher helped Anjum get down her lap and he walked to his seat. The teacher started asking about alphabet to the students in turn.

Anjum answered the teacher quite well. He was getting used to the class environment. He found everything pleasing and entertaining. All his assumptions proved false. He began to develop a liking for his teacher.

Meanwhile the teacher again went to Anjum. He was lost thinking about something. The student sitting beside him shook him. He was startled to see the teacher infront of him. The teacher asked him. "T for....?" Anjum said quickly, "T for teacher." Teacher was very happy. She kissed Anjum's hand.

Anjum was very happy to be loved by the teacher.

A STRANGE GIFT

Amin went to his friend John's house. He was surprised to see the drawing room very well decorated. Beautiful coloured balloons and other decorations were hanging from the ceiling and the walls. There were many funny pictures and paintings on the walls. The chairs were also arranged systematically. A flower vase on the table looked very beautiful.

Amin looked for John everywhere. He followed the smell of sweet dishes and went to the kitchen. There he saw various dishes—cutlets, rasgullas, Pulao, etc.

Seeing so many delicious dishes, his mouth began to water. Then he saw John's mother in the kitchen and asked, "Aunty, where is John?"

It was very difficult for Amin to resist his watering tongue. He was lost visualising the taste of rasgulla. Then only John's mother came out and said. "Today is the birthday of John's elder brother. So, he has gone to market for purchasing gifts for him with his papa."

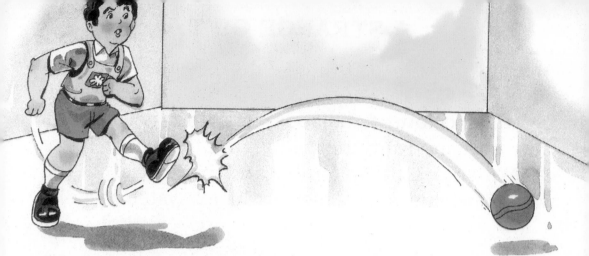

Amin returned home. John is his classmate and a very good friend. They are good neighbours as well. They play football and carrom together.

Amin went into his room. He was not feeling well. Then he went to the garden. He eyes fell on a rose plant which had only one flower. He had planted this rose plant with his own hand. He himself watered the plant daily and also nourished it by fertilizers. He used to sit near the plant seeing it grow beautifully.

Once when Amin was in school his mother had given this rose plant to someone. When Amin came to know about it he got so angry that he refused to eat food until the plant was brought back.

Now sitting before the plant he remembered the past associated with it. Right then he recalled the birthday party of John a month ago, 'How his brother was enjoying his birthday. But my mummy has never celebrated my birthday. I will ask her to celebrate my birthday too.' Amin was lost in his thought.

Now he imagined about his own birthday ceremony like that of John, 'The decorated house with candles and balloons! New clothes! I will be a little king! A big cake, with burning candles on it! I would be blowing off the candles!'

He continued to think ..... 'Mummy will give me cake and people will be singing birthday song and wish me happy birthday. They would be wishing for me to be a doctor, an engineer, a pilot. But how can I be all these together. It is impossible. But I will really have work hard to fulfill the desire of all. I am not afraid of any trouble. Mummy wishes me to be brave, and advises me to face every difficulty. Even Gandhiji was not afraid of English people. He was very brave and I will be like him.'

Staring at the rose plant he was thus lost in day dreaming. All of a sudden he recollected that it was the time of the celebration of David's birthday. He

13

saw people going with gifts to John's house. He thought, 'My mummy will also be there with gifts. I should also take a gift for David. But what should I give to him?' He thought for a while but couldn't decide. Then he calculated the money he had. It was around twenty rupees which did not seem to be sufficient to buy a good present. He cursed himself for not saving enough money.

Then his eyes fell on the rose plant again and he thought, 'What about gifting this plant. I hope it would be better than the gifts of others which will be destroyed sooner or later but the rose plant would continue to grow for years. What an idea!'

He happily rushed to his room and returned with the colour box to the garden and began to paint the vase in different colours.

Sometime later, he heard his mother call him, "Amin! What are you doing? Don't you remember to attend David's birthday party? Come imm- ediately and get ready."

Amin said to her, "Mother you go, I will

be there soon." Then, he got busy in painting the vase again.

After some time, Amin reached David's house with his gift. There were a number of people in the party. David blew off the burning candles and then cut the cake. The room echoed with birthday song "Happy birth day to you...." All the people were served the cake. David was very happy. He was receiving gifts from the people with a smile.

Amin also went to David with his gift. Saying, "Happy birth day to you," he gave his flower vase to David as a birth day gift.

Amin's gift caught everybody's eyes in the party. No body had ever expected such a strange gift.

David said, "Thank you my little brother, I really like your gift very much." Then he picked Amin up and kissed him twice.

Amin was very happy. His face was looking as beautiful as a rose.

OUR DUTY

Deepawali is the festival of lights—the illumination of dark night of *Amavasya*. People express their happiness by putting the lines of lamps, flounces, frills and festoons. The houses look like a hoarding of twinkling stars.

The children are seen in great enthusiasm letting off crackers and enjoying fireworks. Besides the glitter of lights on the earth, the sky is also lit frequently by fired rockets and bombs. It appears as if luminous flowers are falling from the sky.

The faces of the people glow with happiness. With this pleasing atmosphere around, Akash was sitting alone in the lawn of his house. He looked very sad and the dry layers of tears were quite visible on his cheeks. The images of his parents were floating in his eyes. His parents were killed in a road accident a year back. Today he wept for his parents as he was badly missing them on the day of Deepawali. After the death of his parents, Akash had been living with his uncle, Seth Dhani Lal. His uncle treated him as his own son, Arun. On this auspicious day, Arun was firing crackers while Akash was sad. His uncle had given him some of Arun's crackers to Akash.

But when Arun saw his crackers in Akash's hand, he slapped him. Seth Dhani Lal scolded Arun for misbehaving with Akash and sent his servant to buy crackers for Akash.

Akash got relief to see the love of his uncle for him. He remained in the room for a long time which made him feel bored and weary. So, he came out. He was staring at the sky as if he was searching his parents.

He was recollecting his Deepawali days with his parents. He used to decorate the lamps with his mother. His father helped him in fireworks. Sometimes he and his father had arguments. His father liked low sound crackers while Akash preferred those of sharp sound. But his parents used to buy the crackers that he liked. At night when he used to burst the crackers, his parents would warn him to do it carefully. But now only memories were left which, that day were causing him pain with tears rolling down his cheeks.

Suddenly, Akash saw the burning string of a bomb behind Arun. It was about to burst. Unaware of this, Arun was busy in other fireworks. This bomb must be removed otherwise Arun will be hurt badly. Or he must be warned at once. Arun was still busy in burning the bombs.

As Akash was already annoyed with Arun it occurred to him that he should not be saved. This would make him realise how a desperate child like he feels on being hurt.

But Akash was gentle by nature and always treated

others with love and affection. He never thought ill of anyone.

This was the reason which compelled him to give a second thought that shook him–'What are you doing Akash? Arun is your brother. It is your duty to save him from every danger. What happened, if he slapped you. If you behave in the same manner, there will be no difference between you and Arun. It is the time to do your duty. Get up and do your best; follow your conscience.'

Taking it as his duty, Akash quickly got up and thought, 'What should I do? Should I warn Arun or......'

It was already very late and the bomb could burst anytime. In case Akash would call Arun from behind he would see here and there and by that time cracker would have burst. Arun would get hurt. So, only one alternative was left! And Akash did the same. He rushed to the bomb with the speed of a tiger and picked up the cracker to throw away. But before he

could do anything the cracker, it burst in his hand! His hand was burnt.

Hearing the sound of a cracker from behind, Arun turned to Akash. Seeing his hand burnt, Arun understood everything. Akash had taken the risk to save him from the burning cracker. He hung his head out of shame. He had slapped Akash in the afternoon for nothing and Akash burnt his hand to save him.

Arun began to apologize with his hands joined saying, "Forgive me, without any reason I......" He could not speak further. His throat was choked and

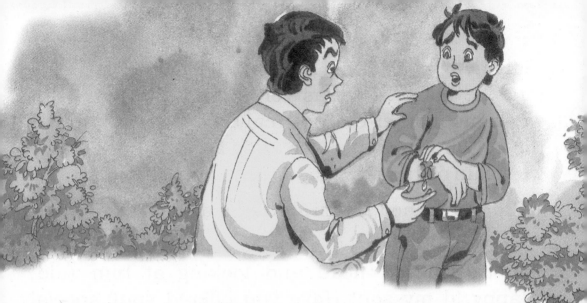

his eyes got wet. Akash only smiled in response. Arun hugged Akash. Tears rolled down his eyes. He continued to say, "How selfish I am! I have always insulted you but you never retaliated, despite being elder to me. You have been nice to me. Now I've realised my mistake."

Hearing Arun, Akash hugged Arun saying, "What are you saying? I just did my duty as a human being."

Then, Arun took Akash in to apply ointment on the wound. Thereafter they both enjoyed bursting of the crackers.

Both Arun and Akash began to live like good brothers. They always played and studied together. They had become inseparable and would never fight. This could be possible only due to sense of duty felt by Akash for his brother Arun.

A REAL REWARD

"Salam Ammijan," said Akram to his mother stepping into the house. He was very happy that day. But when his mother did not reply, he rushed towards the cot on which she was lying and moaning badly with pain on her leg.

"What happened Ammi?" Akram asked his mother, with a worried look.

She turned her head and looking at him said, "Happy Id my son! Have you offered your special prayer of Id?"

"Yes! But what has happened to you?" Akram looked worried to see his mother so ill.

His mother tried to relieve him saying, "Nothing, just a mild pain in the legs. Do not worry. I will be alright soon. Go to

the kitchen and take *seviyan* and other things to eat."

Akram said showing concern for her health, "I have told you so many times not to have so much exertion but you never listen to me."

Akram looked worried. Then he began to massage her mother's feet gently.

It was the day of Id. His mother forced a smile on her face for her son and said, "Don't worry about me, I have only mild pain; it will be alright soon. Today, there is a fair. Take this ten rupee note and enjoy with your friends."

Then Ammi gave him the money saying, "Listen! Today you will also get the reward for the race that you had won."

Akram protested, "No! I will not leave you alone and so sick."

"Why won't you go?" Ammi snubbed him with love.

"Your friends would be waiting ...."

Akram interrupted saying, "I have said that I will not go. That's all. Don't persuade me any further."

Akram continued to massage her feet. He had put the ten rupee note aside. His mother said nothing as she knew that Akram is obstinate and would not listen. She continued to see him with great love.

At that moment, a friend of Akram called him, "Akram! What are you doing? Get ready quickly." It was his friend Shafeek who came to meet him. He was going to the fair.

He came inside after crossing the corridor. He wished *salam* to Akram's mother and said to Akram, "Be quick, the leader is about to come. All friends are waiting for you."

"No, I will not go. Don't you know my mother is ill," said Akram.

"No, my son, I am

alright," said his mother trying to get up from the bed. She continued, "Do not worry about me. Go to the fair with Shafeek and enjoy."

Shafeek too persuaded to Akram but he remained adamant although he was very much eager to go to the fair. Actually he had been waiting for it for a long time but how could he go to the fair leaving his ill mother alone at home.

Finally Shafeek succeeded. He persuaded Akram to go along with him. Akram got up keeping the ten rupee note in his hand. He saw his mother once and moved to the door and then again turned to his mother as if asking for her permission.

His mother said, "I am alright, go without worrying about me."

Akram looked at his mother once again and went outside with Shafeek.

After Akram left for the fair, his mother got lost in

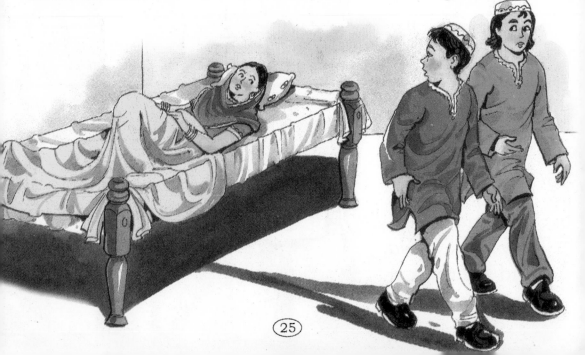

memories of his father . He owned a small grocery shop. He wished to give higher education to Akram but due to low income he could not provide good education to him.

Akram's father had a friend named Hilala who used to send people to foreign countries.

One day, he came to meet Akram's father, Sharafat. Seeing the low income and his intention to give higher education to Akram he said, "Why don't you go to Dubai or somewhere else to earn more so that you can educate your son well and, get rid of your poverty."

Hearing the suggestion of Hilala, Sharafat thought seriously for a while and said, "You are right, but what will I do there? Moreover, I do not have the money to go to Dubai."

Hilala interrupted and said, "Do not worry about the money. I have the *Visa* and there is a vacancy for a

helper. Somehow, make arrangement for the money for the ticket only. After earning you can return my money."

"Do you really mean it?" Sharafat thought his friend was not serious.

"Yes, I do," said Hilala. "Collect the money for the ticket and I will arrange passport etc. for you"

Hearing Hilala, Akram's father jumped with joy. He thanked him and started making arrangements for the money to buy tickets. He tried his best and was able to arrange money for the ticket. Then Sharafat went to Dubai to work as helper.

Recently he had sent some money. Akarm's mother returned some money to the debtor and kept ten rupees for Akram for the Id fair.

It is customary to give some pocket money (idi) to the children on the occasion of Id. If it is not given they would be the victim of inferiority complex.

Suddenly, the legs of Akram's mother began to pain

acutely. When the pain became unbearable, she cried aloud, "Akram!" Surprisingly Akram appeared there. He rushed to his mother and hugged her warmly.

It so happened that while going to the fair he thought of his mother.... 'She may need my help at any moment.... or her condition may become worse.' Thinking this, he turned back. While returning he purchased the medicine for his mother.

He brought a glass of water and gave the medicine to his and said helping his mother to sit up, "Take the medicine."

His mother thought how he managed to purchase the medicine as he had no money. She asked him, "How did you purchase the medicine? Where did you get the money from?"

Akram said, "Ammi you had given me," Saying so he gave the medicine to his mother.

Mother took the medicine. She knew that Akram had not gone to the fair. Then she recollected that Akram was to receive the prize that day. So she said, "You know that you have missed to take your prize."

"No, Ammi," Akram said. "My real prize is to serve you. You have brought me up. I will win more and more prizes with your blessings. You are not feeling well and need my help at this time. How can I go to take the reward leaving you alone in such a condition. You are in pain. How could I go to the fair to be honoured?"

Uttering these words Akram became emotional and tears came in his eyes.

His mother too became emotional. She could not control herself and deep feelings of love and affection for her son turned into tears in her eyes.

SWEET TALKS

You must have seen a little boy running in front of your house. He is none other than the one, who is fat and has a plump body. He looks like a doll. He keeps running here and there all the time; sometime in front of your house and the next moment towards his house. Now you may see him in this street and the next moment in another. He is a live doll and remains busy all the time. His name is Gappoo which means gossip.

Gappoo is very talkative. Though he is just a kid, he talks as if he were older. He enjoys talking with others. He never gets tired of talking but can tire others by his talks. He is called Gappoo only because of his talkative habit. His real name is Shiv Gopal.

Today Gappoo is very happy as his maternal uncle has come to his house. He has brought many toys

and a lot of chocolates. Actually, Gappoo had celebrated his birthday last week. But his maternal uncle could not come on that day because of heavy rainfall. He had conveyed his blessings on phone. Today he has come with many gifts for him.

Gappoo is very happy to have so many toys. Another reason for his happiness is that he can talk to his uncle for hours without any interruption. He did not want to lose this opportunity. His aunty had already told him that his uncle would come next week.

Since then, he has thought of the topics on which he wanted to talk to his maternal uncle.

His father goes to office in the morning and comes back late in the evening. His brother remains busy in his studies. Therefore he has no one with whom he could gossip. When he goes out of the house, to his friends, his mother punishes him with the

warning, "Gopi do not wander outside for a long time. You will be spoiled roaming with dirty boys."

How could he say that he gets bored alone in the house having no one to talk? Mother remains busy all the time with household work. He has no company whom he can talk with. How to pass the time is a big problem for him.

Today when his maternal uncle came his joy knew no bounds. The best thing is that his uncle takes interest in his talks. But even his uncle seems to get tired of this soon. But Gappoo is never tired of talking. He can talk whole day and night without any break or rest.

Gappoo is known by three names. In school, he is called Shiv Gopal, friends call him Gappoo while the parents call him Gopi.

His mother went to the kitchen to prepare tea for her brother. But there was no milk. She called, "Gopi! Go and call your brother to bring milk for tea."

But Gappoo did not want to leave his uncle. He got angry with his mother. "Whenever I talk to someone mummy in-terrupts all the time and asks to do this work or that work," Gappoo murmured looking at his maternal uncle. "Now tell me, how do you feel, if someone disturbs you

when you are doing your favourite job. Will you not mind it? Even mummy will mind if some one disturbs her during her favourite serial or movie."

Gappoo was enjoying talking with his maternal uncle but his mother disturbed him by asking him to call his brother. This spoiled his mood. He got upset feeling the same way, like when the cartoon film on T.V. is disturbed. Gappoo looked at his mother carelessly and said aloud, "Where is brother?"

"See, he must be somewhere outside," said his mother.

Gappoo said nothing and went out reluctantly. His mother and uncle smiled to see him go outside. He went to a park but instead of looking for his brother he saw four puppies playing with their mother. He was lost in seeing them and forgot the purpose of his coming out.

The bitch was lying on the grass and the puppies were jumping over her. Gappoo wished to play with the puppies but as he approached them the bitch started barking at him. He got scared and ran for his life.

Thereafter Gappoo reached the flower bed in the park. He liked the coloured flowers. Suddenly, a butterfly came into his sight there and started sucking the juice of the flowers. Gappoo was very happy to see the butterfly and tried to catch her.

The butterfly was very hungry. She was satisfying her hunger by taking nectar from the flowers. She did not like the disturbance and so she made

faces at Gappoo as if she was refusing to have sweet talks with him. Soon she disappeared behind the bushes.

To see this, Gappoo got upset with the butterfly. He cursed her very much and went near a tree.

Gappoo saw a nest on the tree. There were many newly born chicks in the nest. They all were chirping a lot.

Gappoo went near the nest. As the chicks saw him, they raised their voice due to fear. Their mother was not present at that time. Gappoo was very happy as he had got the opportunity to talk and play with the chicks. He did not want to waste this opportunity. As he extended his hand to pick one of the chicks, their mother came. When she saw Gappoo near the nest she cried at the top of her voice and started pecking at him with her beak.

Gappoo did not like the way the bird behaved. Abusing the bird he moved ahead.

By that time Gappoo had already forgotten the work assigned to him by his mother. Now as he had nothing to do, he sat down on the ground. Then, he saw the same bitch in the park. She went to her pups to feed them.

Gappoo thought, 'Every one is busy in his work and no one has the time to talk with me. It appears that I am the only worthless fellow. I saw that the bitch, butterfly, bird were busy in their respective works. But what about me! Even I should have done something by now." Then he recollected, "Mother had sent me to look for the brother! But I am here........"

Gappoo glanced here and there but he could not see his brother. He returned home. He thought,

'It is very late. Mother will scold me a lot. She would not have made tea yet for *mamaji*.'

As soon as he entered the house, he heard his mother, "Gopi...?"

Gopi became nervous to hear his mother. He went to mother slowly. Mummy lost her temper and asked in anger, "Where have been for so long? I have been waiting for you but your were nowhere to be found."

Hearing his mother, Gopi came to her weeping and said with tears in his eyes, "I will never come late in future. Nor will I gossip in future and waste time."

Gopi's innocent words dispelled mother's anger. She smiled and picked Gopi up in her arms, caressing his head. She was no longer upset with Gopi.

A GREAT LESSON

No sooner did our last period of Hindi got over, than all the boys rushed towards gate in a fit of excitement and freedom. As I was just collecting my books a boy pushed me and one of my books fell on the floor. I got annoyed and looked here and there for the boy but found none. As I was about to pick up my book, I saw an envelope lying on the floor. Out of curiousity I picked it up and opened. There were marksheets of High School and Intermediate of some boy. Putting them back in the envelope, I smiled.

I was a student of B.A. first year. Often we used to hide the personal things of some student and would return him only after receiving a treat. Though it was all wrong yet we enjoyed having fun.

The marksheet belonged to a boy named Mansukha. He was searching for them anxiously. He was very frustrated. Seeing the envelope in my hand, he understood everything. He came to me and said,

"Dear brother, kindly return my papers."

"But they are not yours!" I said rudely.

Hearing my words, he got nervous. After some time, he spoke again "Give me the envelope, these are my marksheets in it."

"Okay, it is yours! But how did it come in my hands?"

Now one of my friends said, " Listen my dear! It is yours and important as well. If it was lost it would cost you a lot of money and time."

Mansukha said, "You are right." "But we will solve your problem in twenty rupees only," said another friend. "Give us a treat and take the envelope. Am I right?"

"Why not?" I said compromisingly. "We are interested only in the treat. We have nothing to do with your certificate."

"But I have only ten rupees Sajid Bhai," saying this he folded his hand.

"All right!" we said, "We will manage the rest. Let's go to the restaurant."

"Oh yes! Why not?" He gave a forced smile.

We all walked towards the hotel. On reaching the hotel we enjoyed the treat and came back to the college.

When in the class I needed the pen to write something. I found it missing. It was made of silver with an electronic watch. This costly pen was presented to me on my birthday by my maternal uncle. My mother had already warned me against taking that costly silver pen to the college on fear of being lost.

As I wanted to impress my friends, I ignored her warning. Now, what would I do?

Mother and father would be angry with me for my carelessness. Really, if I had obeyed them, I would not have to face such an awkward situation. During the class I felt restless and looked here and there for the lost pen. The teacher took it for my not being serious to the class and scolded me. I remained restlessly silent till the period was over. I was very frustrated at that time.

I started looking for my lost pen. I asked all the friends about it but to no avail. "Sajid, is it your pen?" I heard a voice from behind. As I turned to the voice, I saw Mansukha with my pen in his hand. He was the same boy whom we had forced to treat us just for returning his own marksheets.

I thought that he would certainly be in a retaliating mood and would ask for a treat. He might be adamant for a large treat for returning that costly pen.

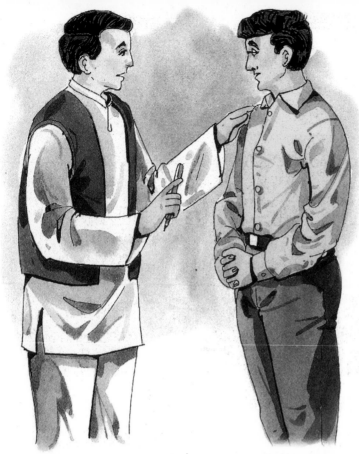

He came near me and putting his hand around my shoulder, said, "Take your pen dear! I found it lying behind your seat. But if you do not mind, I would suggest you not to bring such expensive things to the college."

I was surprised to see his behaviour. It was quite unexpected! I was brought up in the city while he belonged to a rural area. He was quite innocent but intelligent in studies despite lacking the facilities that I enjoyed. But he had a great respect for human values which I lacked even if unknowingly.

I was ashamed of myself for my attitude when I saw him in trouble. At the same time I was much impressed to see his gentle and unrevengeful attitude. I in his place would have teased and forced to have treat. As I turned to Mansukha to thank and regret my action, he was not there. I shall ever be thankful to him for teaching me this great lesson of humanity.

DEBT OF FRIENDS

It was five o'clock in the evening. Aslam was alone in his room. He had just returned from the playground. He cast a glance at the kitchen and found his mother and sister busy in cooking. His father was in the bathroom at that time. Nobody had seen Aslam come inside the house. He used to go out and come in often without being seen by anyone.

Aslam reached the clothes peg like a hunting cat. He found his father's pants hanging there. Quickly he felt inside the pocket. His heart was beating fast!

Next moment the heavy purse was in his hand. Out of fear, he felt the presence of his father behind him.

He turned immediately but there was no one. It was just his false doubt. He thought, 'If it is not done now, I will never get such an opportunity in future.'

Aslam hurriedly opened the purse. It was

filled with the notes of five hundred and one hundred. Aslam quickly took out a note. It was a one hundred rupee note. He needed it badly. He put the purse back in the pocket. His bag was also lying there. He took out a book from the bag, put the note in it and then kept the book back in the bag. Thereafter, he slipped outside the house.

The boys were waiting eagerly in the playground. One of them said, "Aslam, where were you? Come." But Aslam refused.

The boys kept on playing. Aslam sat on a bench in the park. His heartbeats were still beating fast out of fear. He was planning to return the money he had borrowed from his friends the other day.

Thus, he would be saved from their threats. Next moment he thought about the hundred rupee note. He was thinking that he should not have put the note in the bag as someone might open the bag and would be caught. Then his father would punish him by beating and scolding. Even his mother would scold him badly. It would also make them sad to know that their son had a bad habit of stealing. They would never believe him again and he would lose their confidence forever.

He was filled with inferiority complex for what he had done. He was now regretting his act of borrowing from his friends for enjoying spicy dishes. Now he felt that at any cost he should not have stolen money, even if his friends would complain to his father. At least he would not lose confidence of his parents. Now if his theft was caught, the parents would never believe him.

Next moment Aslam decided to repent for his wrong deed. He thought that he would tell everything to his father. At least he would retain his confidence and would feel proud of telling the truth. With this determination he walked towards home.

When he reached home he saw his father reading a book in his room. It occurred to him that his father might have caught his theft. But he still

wanted to tell the truth in all circumstances. He reached his father with firm determination and said, "Father, I want to tell you something."

"Yes, what is that?" said his father looking at him.

"I want you to punish me!" Aslam said with hesitation.

His father was astonished to hear him say so as he was still unaware of the theft. So he asked Aslam, "Why should I punish you? What wrong have you done?"

"I have stolen money from your purse", saying so he took out the hundred rupee note from the book and put it in front of his father.

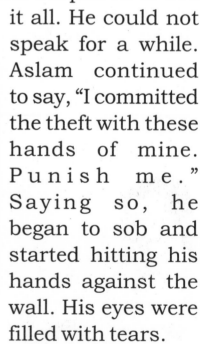

His father was surprised to see it all. He could not speak for a while. Aslam continued to say, "I committed the theft with these hands of mine. Punish me." Saying so, he began to sob and started hitting his hands against the wall. His eyes were filled with tears.

Now his father understood everything. He

consoled Aslam, saying, "Don't cry, my son." Aslam was looking at his father with the feeling of guilt.

"Listen!" his father continued, "The biggest punishment is repentance. If you realise that you have committed something wrong and want to reform yourself, then what is the need of punishment? Punishment is for reforming a wrongdoer. I am not hurt for your committing the theft. On the contrary I am happy to know that you realized that it was wrong. But, I want to know why you needed to steal the money what would you have done with that money? There must be some reason behind it."

Aslam was encouraged by the words of his father. "I had borrowed from my friends to buy some eatables. They were asking me frequently to return the money. They also threatened to make complaints to you. So being scared of their threats I stole the money from your purse." Having said so, Aslam felt too ashamed of himself to even to look at his father's face. He stood with his head down.

"Now forget about it," said his father patting on Aslam's back.

Aslam promised his father that he would never repeat it in future. Nor would he ever borrow from anybody.

Then his father said, "It is all right. I appreciate you for speaking the truth. Take this hundred rupee note and return the money to your friends."

Aslam took the note with a little hesitation and kept it in his pocket.

This time he was not afraid of keeping the note as it was given to him in a respectable manner.

Next day he went to his friends and returned the money. Thus, confessing our wrongdoings, prevents us from committing them any more.

DISTRIBUTOR OF PRASAD

In the evening Garima was playing hide and seek with her brother Gaurav. She went to the gate and stood there with her eyes closed facing outside the gate. She started counting... "one, two, three...."

After counting up to ten she shouted, "Brother, should I come now?"

"Yes! Come," shouted Gaurav. Then Garima opened her eyes and started searching for her brother.

First of all she went towards the earthen pots of flowers, but Gaurav was not there. Then she peeped behind the pipes, and looked around the pillars in the veranda. But Gaurav was not there. She stood, trying to guess where he must be, then suddenly, an idea struck her mind! She cried aloud, "Papa has come!"

To her amazement, she heard the sound of the bike.

Gaurav also came out from behind one of the pillars. They both rushed together to open the gate. But Garima was surprised of the coincidence. How her father came on the scene? Motor cycle stopped near the gate. Both the children climbed on the bike. When their father stopped the bike in the veranda, they got down.

"Papa, what have you brought for us?" asked Garima and Gaurav together.

Everyday they waited for their father in the evening to return and would enjoy their favourite things that he never missed to bring.

Garima is a pretty girl who looked like a doll with round face, short cut hair, pearl like teeth, and an everlasting smile on her face. When she smiles her teeth look like the dew drops on the petals of rose shining in the sunlight. Her innocent face with agile movements of eyes attracts everyone.

That day their papa had brought biscuits for them. But Gaurav snatched it from his father's hand and ran into the house leaving his sister crying. Even while weeping Garima looked very attractive. Her papa picked her up in his arms and wiped the tears from her eyes saying, "Oh no, Garima is a nice girl. She never weeps."

Garima said sobbingly, "First give me my packet of biscuits."

"I am just giving you that," said her papa and called Gaurav to bring the packet to him.

Garima turned to look towards the door.

After some time, Gaurav came there walking slowly with the packet of biscuits in his hand.

Gaurav said nothing but extended the packet of biscuits to his father. Seeing the packet, Garima smiled. Papa took the packet and said to Gaurav, "Why are you looking so sad? You will also get your share." Then he turned to Garima and said, "Won't you give the *prasad* to your brother after offering it to the God in the temple."

Garima instantly said, "Yes! I will?" Papa handed over the packet to Garima and went to change his clothes. Garima inspected the packet minutely. When she was sure that it was not opened by Gaurav she opened it.

There was a temple near her house. Garima used to go to the temple daily not to worship the God but for the sweets she got from the priest. Once she asked the priest, "Why do you distribute the *prasad* to the people? Don't you like the sweets?"

"I like the sweets very much," the priest said looking affectionately at her. "The *prasad* of the God is

meant to be distributed among the devotees. If it is not distributed, the God will get annoyed. And too much sweets also spoil the teeth."

Since then Garima believed firmly that distribution of *prasad* pleases the God. Therefore, she always distributes the sweets as prasad.

Garima opened the packet and counted the biscuits. They were twenty. She gave five biscuits to her brother saying, "Take your prasad."

When Gaurav asked for more, she said, "No, *prasad* will be distributed to all. Papa and mummy will also

get prasad." Saying this she went to the kitchen.

Her mother was busy in the kitchen. Garima gave five biscuits to her mother as prasad. Her mother said, "Eat yourself."

But Garima was ready with her reply, "Mummy, it is *prasad*. Take it otherwise the God will get angry." Her mother smiled and said, "Don't you see that my hands are dirty and *prasad* should not be taken with dirty hands; so you have them."

Garima agreed. Then she went outside the house where children were waiting for her. They knew that Garima had come to distribute the *prasad* as usual.

Seeing Garima the children cried, "Give us *prasad*." Garima felt proud of herself and distributed all the biscuits except one.

All the children went to their houses. She had only one biscuit left for herself.

But as she was about to put the biscuit in her mouth, her brother came running and said, "Garima, my share?"

Hearing her brother, she stopped her hand and asked him, "Haven't you got the *prasad*?"

She did not remember if she had given him his share or not. Hence she asked her brother, "Have you really not got t h e *prasad*?"

Hearing her sister, he hesitated a bit as he had already taken his share. But he moved his head in negation.

Garima could not understand his trick to get more. Only one biscuit was left with her and that too her favourite. She thought if she ate the last biscuit without giving it as *prasad* to her brother, then God would be annoyed. So she gave the biscuit to her brother.

Gaurav quickly grabbed the biscuit lest she should change her mind or his cleverness might be caught. He was very happy as his trick had worked. He was enjoying the biscuit while Garima was watching him.

Garima had distributed all the biscuits as *parsad*. She got nothing, but her face was shining. She looked happier having distributed the *prasad* to others than Gaurav who had played a trick on her.

A ROSE FLOWER

No sooner did Golu opened his eyes than he sighted the flowers made of plastic on the Almirah. His round cheeks turned red like the rose flower. He rushed to the little garden in front of the veranda.

There were different types of flowers in the garden. Besides, there were many flower pots put along the wall. But ahead of these flower pots there was a small pot of a rose plant in the corner of the garden. Golu went straight to that rose plant.

He observed the rose plant minutely. There was a beautiful rose blossomed on it. There were dew drops on the petals of the rose which were shining like pearls in the sunlight. He touched a drop and smiled. But then he thought not to touch the other drops as the flower looked more beautiful with the dew drops.

Happy and gay, Golu smelt the rose. The fragrance was several times better than the smell of Chocolates and sweets. Smelling the sweet fragrance of the rose

Golu could not help himself feeling it on his cheek.

The soft touch of the rose brightened his face which appeared redder than the rose itself. He felt tickly and smiled. His milky teeth were shining like pearls. The joy of Golu knew no bound. There were ripples of happiness in his eyes. A sweet smile appeared on his reddish lips like rose petals. He was thrilled to see the beauty of nature.

The little rose pleased him more than the toys his moving train or dolls made of rubber or cartoon films on the T.V. etc.

At this moment a colourful butterfly appeared there. First, he became happy to see the butterfly, but when he saw the butterfly moving towards his favourite rose, he became alert. He would not tolerate anyone to smell his rose. Hence he decided not to allow the butterfly to sit on the rose.

He murmured, "Oh! The butterfly is greedy . She has not yet washed its mouth. How she dared come here so early in the morning to impure my favourite rose." And the next moment Golu rushed towards the butterfly to make her fly.

But the butterfly did not go anywhere. She kept on flying around the rose as if she was determined to suck the nectar of the flower. On the other hand, Golu was determined to make the butterfly fly away from his garden.

Golu got tired of running after the butterfly. The palpitation of his heart increased considerably and he started breathing fast. Sweat also appeared on his face. Finally, he sat under a tree to take rest. As the cold breeze touched his body, he felt comforted. He thought, 'It is the nature of a butterfly to sit on flowers. If I do not allow it to suck the nectar, where will it go. It will remain hungry for the whole day. It

will suffer the whole day only because of me?'

Hence his anger vanished and he looked at the butterfly with great affection. She was sitting on another plant but her eyes were still on the rose. Since Golu had changed his mind he said to the butterfly, "You seem to be angry with me. Well, come and smell the rose." But the butterfly did not move. Golu thought, 'She is very angry with me. After all I must have tired her a lot. I am really very naughty and always tease others. I should apologize to her.'

Then, he folded his hands and said, "I am sorry. Come and smell the rose. Oh, it appears you are still angry. Please believe me. I am really sorry." But the butterfly still remained in the same position.

Now it occurred to Golu that the butterfly must be feeling shy. So he put his hands over his eyes to cover them.

But he continued to see through his fingers. The butterfly did not move. It remained stuck to the

plant. Then Golu opened his eyes and said, "I think you know that you are being observed. Okey, now I turn my back to you." After some time when he turned back, he saw the butterfly in the same position.

To see this, Golu said, "It is alright. Now I am going from here." Then he walked towards his home but returned after some time. As he turned his back he found that the butterfly was sitting on the rose. She was sucking the nectar freely.

The butterfly moved her wings twice as if she was expressing her gratitude and saying "Thank you." Golu also waved his hands and said, "Good Bye."

Now Golu was feeling happier. He also learnt a lesson that 'one should not disturb any creature'.

I AM INDEPENDENT

Ahal was very happy that day. After all his birthday was being celebrated. The house was decorated with buntings and strings of bulbs. His mother had prepared a lot of dishes for the party. He had been enjoying the smell of these dishes since morning. The house had been full of guests throughout the day. As soon as Ahal blew off the candles on the cake, everybody clapped. Then he cut the cake which was distributed among the guests.

Ahal received the gifts from his guests with a smile on his face. The gifts included football, bat-ball, mouth organ, chocolates, ship, battery operated rocket etc.

But what he liked most was a colourful book. He went to his room with the book and tried to know its contents. It was a story book. There were colourful pictures with every story, he turned the pages and opened the first story. The title was 'The Price of Freedom.' Reading the title he was perplexed. He did not know the meaning of the freedom.

He got up, and went straight to the kitchen where mummy was busy cleaning. Seeing Ahal she said, "Do not come here, I have yet to clean the kitchen. Go to your room." Ahal stopped at the gate and said, "But, mummy, I have to ask something."

As mummy was busy working in the kitchen, she said, "Go to papa and ask him."

Ahal was disturbed for a moment but then he saw his father who was arranging the chairs in the veranda.

Ahal went upto him and said, "May I take your one minute?"

His father saw him with a surprise and said, "Tell me what you want."

Ahal at once said, "What is freedom?"

His father looked at him and said, "Freedom means independence and liberty. You know that our country was not free but now we are free."

Hearing his father he could not understand the meaning and started itching his head.

Papa was in a fix. He was not able to convince his son about the meaning of freedom. Still he wanted to make him understand the meaning of freedom.

Suddenly, his father saw a mouse who was running here and there. He pointed to it and said, "Do you see the mouse? It goes wherever it wants. None stops it, nor does it have to ask anyone where to go and what to do. This is called freedom."

Ajay was thrilled with such a wonderful idea of freedom. He murmured. "Oh! What a nice thing the freedom is. To do what you like! To go where you want! And needn't ask anyone!"

Ahal said curiously, "Papa, do I also have freedom?"

"Why not? All are free in our country, so are you. Now go to your room, I want to arrange these chairs."

Ahal went to his room, put the book aside and sat on the chair. His joy knew no bound to know the wonderful thing like freedom which he already had but was not aware of it till now. His mind was working fast. He thought, "I will also enjoy the freedom by doing anything that pleases me." Then he remembered the sweets kept in the kitchen.

He was not happy as only two pieces were given to him. he went inside the kitchen and saw the jar of sweets on an upper shelf.

Anyway, he would use the tin can of flour to reach

the jar. But when he tried to pick the jar his balance was disturbed and the jar fell on the ground with a loud noise and broke into pieces.

Hearing the sound his mother came rushing to the kitchen. She saw that sweets were scattered all around the

floor. She lost her temper and scolded her son Ahal for untidying the kitchen. She said, "You have become very naughty these days. You have also spoiled the sweets. If you wanted to eat the sweets, why didn't you ask me for it? I would have given you."

The poor fellow remained silent and stood with his head down. He was badly confused about the concept of freedom!

Seeing the mother busy in cleaning he slipped from there and went straight to his room.

Suddenly, he picked up the remote control and switched on the TV.

Just then, his elder brother came there and scolded Ahal, "Why do you keep the volume so high? Don't you know that I am preparing for my exam?"

Saying so, he closed the TV. Ahal was sad for not able to enjoy cartoon show and was constantly thinking about the sort of freedom he had. I cannot eat sweet, nor can I watch the TV still they say that I have freedom.

Suddenly, he saw a football lying in the room. Now he wanted to keep on kicking the football till he would lose his annoyance. He jumped from his seat, picked up the football and went to play outside the room.

He kicked the football as forcibly as if it had created the hurdles on the way of his freedom. Having kicked the football he felt much relieved. But, the next moment he saw that the

football had directly hit his father's face and his specs fell down on the ground.

Ahal now knew that after the mother and brother it was his father's turn to scold him for enjoying his freedom. But fortunately it did not happen. His father came to Ahal and said in a very soothing manner "What is the matter? Have you any problem?"

"No papa, nothing... I was just...." Ahal began to falter.

His father came near him and said, "Don't worry my son. My specs are fine.

But let me know what is wrong with you. You are looking annoyed. Has your mummy scolded you?"

"Papa, I was not doing anything wrong. I was doing the things

as I wished. Didn't you tell that this is what is freedom. And I have freedom?"

Papa interrupted with a smile on his face and said, "You are right that you have freedom to do anything you like. But it doesn't mean that you should not care about others. Your action should not disturb and bother others. If it happens, then it is a misuse of the freedom for which you can be punished as well."

"Yes papa," said Ahal, "now I understood freedom very well. In future I will not let others suffer by whatever I do." Then, Ahal ran towards his football and was about to kick it. But he stopped and saw around to make sure that it would not hit anyone. Then he kicked the football. His father was smiling at him.

SWEET MANGOES

When the little girl, Gudia and his elder brother Arif were about to enter the house, they heard the pigeons uttering 'Gutergoo-Gutergoo' as if they were welcoming them. Sitting on the thatched roof and moving their heads they seemed to be welcoming a queen. Seeing pigeons Gudia was pleased very much. Her cheeks turned reddish. She smiled waving her little hands towards the pigeons.

Gudia had come to meet her elder sister with her brother, Arif. Seeing Gudia, her sister was very happy. She held her in her arms affectionately and said after kissing her cheeks, "Oh, my sweet Gudia! How are you?"

Gudia looked shy and smiled without saying anything.

Then her sister

served them cold drinks and snacks. Having finished with it, Arif lay down on the cot. Being tired, soon he fell asleep. But Gudia did not sleep. She kept on looking here and there and happened to see a half ripe mango in the room.

The sight of the mango made her mouth water. She was so fond of mangoes that she would not dislike even sour ones.

Gudia woke up her brother. Being disturbed in this manner he got angry and said, "What is the matter? Why don't you let me sleep?"

Seeing her brother upset, she did not speak anything but pointed towards the Mango. This irritated him but before he could say anything, their sister brought a basket full of washed mangoes. She put the basket before them saying, "These are very tasty mangoes for you to eat."

Both of them began to enjoy the mangoes. Sitting near them their sister asked them about other people at home. Both the children ate the mangoes as much as they could and sat on the cot. Then Gudia asked about her *jijaji* (brother-in-law). Her sister told that he was in the orchard. Then she called a boy and sent them to the orchard with him.

They were very happy to visit their sister. Now, Gudia wanted to give a surprise to her *jijaji*.

There were trees all over. The mangoes were hanging so low that even a child could pluck them easily. The mangoes on the trees were alluring to Gudia. She could pluck some but she was afraid of Arif.

Then she saw her *jijaji* and rushed to him. He picked her up in his arms affectionately.

Then Arif also reached them. He greeted him

respectfully. His *jijaji* asked the well being of his in-laws. The conversation between them was quite boring for Gudia and she got off her jijaji's arms.

Jijaji asked her if she would like to eat mangoes. But before Gudia could express her desire, Arif interrupted, "We have already had more than enough at home."

"Well, let us take a round of the garden. This will help you digest the mangoes you have eaten," said jijaji and put the basket of mangoes in a hut in the garden.

The children followed their jijaji. Suddenly Arif asked in a surprise, "What is that on the mangoes like white powder?"

His jijaji said, "These are *Banarasi* mangoes and the white powder is like their make up which is why they are costly."

"But who applies the powder on them?" asked Gudia.

"Nobody. It is natural." said jijaji".

"Then it must need a good care," said Arif.

His jijaji said, "Yes, it is plucked with its twig."

Meanwhile, a mango dropped from the tree. Their Jijaji gave it to Gudia and proceeded ahead.

All of a sudden, Arif saw a cuckoo on a tree. "Gudia see, there is a cuckoo!" Arif turned to Gudia, but she was nowhere to be seen. Arif was astonished. He ran towards the hut followed by his jijaji.

They reached the hut calling, "Gudia! Gudia! Where are you?" Gudia was eating mangoes sitting on the cot inside the hut. Gudia gave them her naughty smile.

Arif frowned at her and said, "Gudia! What is all this?"

Gudia stopped eating and looking at Arif said innocently, "Dear brother! How sweet these mangoes are! Just taste one and you will want to finish all."

Seeing her innocent face, Arif and jijaji both burst into laughter. Gudia looked at them with an innocent surprise and paused a bit to see as to why they were laughing. Then she began to eat the mango again.

A PROMISE OF A FAIRY

Karim was sitting in the lawn. Suddenly his eyes fell on a beautiful rose on a small plant. Karim got charmed by its mere sight and rushed to pluck it. Before he could reach the plant, he stopped suddenly on hearing a cry, "Help! Help!" He was surprised to hear the cry! He wondered where the voice was coming from. There was a pond nearby. The voice seemed to be coming from that direction. Immediately he reached there and saw a fairy there who was weeping.

He had read about the fairy in the book only. But now there was one before his eyes. She had white face, golden hair, cotton like wings and silky dress. Now Karim felt scared too as he had read that fairies have magical power to change anyone into a bird or something else. But that fairy was weeping!

Karim went near her and asked, "Why are you crying?" "My stick has fallen into the pond," said the fairy, "and I cannot return without it." She, then, pointed towards the stick in the pond.

Karim saw a golden stick in the pond. He wasted no time and jumped into the water and brought the stick back after some time. He gave the golden stick to the fairy.

The fairy was very happy to get her stick back.

She thanked Karim very much saying, "I will always be thankful to you." She kissed the stick and looking at Karim she said, "If you wish I can take you to my country, the country of fairies."

"Is it possible?" he asked and thought, 'If it is so, I will be the first man to visit the fairyland'. Karim nodded his head in affirmation. He said, "Yes! I will go with you."

"All right, I will take you there," said the fairy. She caught his hand and flew in the sky. He

was enjoying the voyage to the fairyland.

Soon they reached above the clouds. Karim saw that clouds looked like cotton. He was very happy.

Suddenly, he saw a shining object in the sky. The fairy told it was the gate of the fairy land. Soon they entered the fairy land.

Karim could smell floral fragrance all around. He was very happy. He moved here and there. There were beautiful trees all over the land with colourful flowers.

The leaves shone like the burning bulbs and instead of fruits he was surprised to see biscuits, toffees, chocolates, etc. on the trees. These were trees of eatables just like fruit. It was an extraordinary experience for Karim. Then the fairy said to Karim, "You should not touch any of the things you see here."

"Okay," said Karim assuring the fairy.

As they went ahead he saw the trees of sweets. All types of sweets Rasagulla, laddu, barfi, etc. were hanging on the tree. The sight of sweets on the trees watered his mouth.

Then he saw the trees of money. The notes of all sort were on the trees like leaves. He had imagined all about this one year ago and hence sowed one rupee coin in the ground hoping to get a money tree but there was none. But in the fairy land he could actually see them.

There were several mountains made of butter on one side. There were springs of milk as well. Besides, there were lakes of curd and *ghee.* Karim was astonished to see the fairy land where anybody could eat as much as he wanted. But the fairy did not let him eat anything. His mouth was watering and he had to gulp it down.

Meanwhile the queen of fairy happened to pass in her chariot. The fairy bowed with respect to the queen. But when she saw Karim she said, "Who has brought this naughty boy to the fairy land? He will spoil our trees. Send him back immediately or he will ruin our beautiful land." Saying this, the queen went ahead.

Hearing the queen, the fairy asked Karim, "Did you hear the queen's order? Now you will have to go."

Karim was disappointed to hear the words of fairy. He requested her, "Please allow me to stay here for some days more."

The fairy saw that Karim was sad. She said, "If you treat the plants as your friends and promise to protect them, I will persuade the queen to let you stay."

Karim got so happy to hear the fairy and promised never to harm any plants. He wanted to spend some more time in the fairy land.

"All right!" said the fairy. "Now go back I will call you here soon". Then she moved her magic stick around Karim.

Karim felt as if he was thrown down on the earth .He closed his eyes out of fear. When he opened his eyes he found himself on the bed in his room.

It was holiday and he was lying on bed, dreaming late in the morning. Now his dream was over.

But he remembered his promise made to the fairy that he would never harm the plants and would protect them instead.

A FRIEND OF DREAMS

Lalit was very happy that day. There had been a strange shine on his face since he got up in the morning. His cheeks had become red and he had a fixed smile on his lips.

The reason of his happiness was the arrival of his friend. His friend was not an ordinary person. She was very important and loving too. She was of the same age as Lalit, but was much more beautiful than the moon. When she laughed, it appeared that pearls were falling from her mouth. And when she sang all the animals of the earth lost senses and danced on the tune of her magical song.

Naturally, it could not be a human but a fairy and for sure his friend was a fairy. A real fairy! Do you know how and where Lalit met her. No. All right! I

will tell you. But do not laugh, Lalit met her in his dreams. Their meeting occurred unexpectedly as when a guest comes to our house. Exactly in the same manner, she came in his dream as a guest and he welcomed her.

It was only yesterday when Lalit was plucking flowers in the garden. Just then the fairy came there and said to Lalit, "What are you doing? Do you not know that plucking flowers pain the plant and them the flowers also die."

Lalit said, "I am sorry. I promise that I will not pluck flowers in future."

Fairy smiled and said, "Never forget your promise."

"Okay! But will you like to have friendship with me?"
"Why? Don't you have any friend"? asked the fairy.

"No, I have no friend!"
Lalit said.

Actually, Lalit was a very naughty boy. He was in the first standard. But he did not like to study. He like playing games, wandering here and there, eating spicy food and watching TV. Seeing him careless other students avoided his company. He

remained busy all day in his mischiefs.

"All right! I accept your friendship," said the fairy. She extended her hand to him. Lalit happily shook hands with the fairy and they began to play together.

At this moment his mother woke Lalit up. He told his mother about his dream. He also told about the dream to his sister and brother. Thereafter he went to school and boasted for having friendship with a fairy.

Lalit passed his day happily thinking about the fairy. Now he named her as Little Fairy. Since she was very small the name suited her.

The friendship between Lalit and the fairy deepened further. Lalit roamed about with the fairy all night in his dreams.

One day, Lalit did not go to school. He made an excuse of having stomach ache. His mother gave him medicine and asked him to take rest. Lalit also

wished the same. He went to the bed and lay down on it to sleep so that he could enjoy the company of the fairy in his dream.

Thinking about the fairy he fell asleep.

Soon, Lalit was lost in the colourful world of dreams. He went to the home of the fairy. But she was not home. He was disappointed and started calling her name loudly.

Suddenly, a parrot appeared there and told Lalit that the fairy had gone to school. Then the parrot flew away. Now Lalit decided to go to the school to find if the parrot was not lying.'

Then, he reached the school of fairies. He saw that there were many fairies in the school. He searched for his Little Fairy. When he saw her, he smiled and hinted her to come out of the class.

She came out of the class and said, "What is the matter? Why have you come here? Did you not go to the school today?"

Lalit said, "No, I do not like school at all." Little Fairy became sad to hear Lalit. She further said, "You have not done right. It is the time for you to study hard."

"But I do not like to study," said Lalit.

Little Fairy thought a little and said, "Well, Lalit, are you my true friend or not?"

"Of course, I am your true friend," Lalit said happily. "Then don't you think that after studying I should progress and become a great person to earn name and fame?"

"Yes! Yes! Why not?" Lalit said hesitantly.

"In the same way, I wish for you my friend that you should also progress after studying hard. Even your parents think the same. Will you not like to fulfill their and my dreams?" She peeped in the eyes of Lalit. "Tell me, will you?" Fairy motivated Lalit.

Lalit assured her and said, "Yes! I will do that."

Hearing this, Little Fairy smiled. Her small cheeks blushed. All of a sudden, Lalit woke up. He recollected his promise made to his friend . He thought for a while. Then he washed his mouth and hands and went to his room to study with conviction.

FIRST DAY AT SCHOOL

It was Bano's first day in the school. She had gone to school with her sister. It had taken enough time to get Bano ready for school. As a result she got late. Her sister took Bano to the class and told her, "This is your class. Take your seat. Your teacher is about to come. I am getting late so......."

"All right!" Bano said slowly.

Her sister then went to her class.

Bano opened the door of the class and peeped inside to ensure that there was no cat. She was very afraid of cats. She became happy to see several children of the same age together in the class. Now, she was no longer afraid of cat.

Suddenly some of the children started crying. Bano became very angry and thought, 'These children are very naughty. They do not know how to sit in the class. Look at me! I came to school for the first time but I did not cry at all. These are dirty children.'

Bano, holding her bag, entered the class. She was about to scold them but they themselves stopped crying. She was surprised to see the whole class. There were so many children together at a place. At home she played with her four cousins but here she was among more than 30 children in one room.

Then a boy from the front seat got up and came up to her. He moved her hand slowly and spoke in a lisping voice, "Will you be my friend?" The boy wanted to be the first to win her friendship in the class. Moreover, he had just broken up with his best friend so when he saw Bano–he walked upto her and asked her whether she would be her friend.

Bano also replied in a sweet lisping, voice with a smile on her face. "Yes! I will."

Both smiled and shook hands. The class witnessed the whole episode.

But before they could ask each other's names, the teacher came into the class. They rushed to their respective seats. The teacher took the attendance.

Then casting a glance to the whole class, she began to teach.

"A for apple. Apple means......"

As Bano heard the word 'apple' her mouth began to water, she liked apple very much. Her papa also used to say, "The red cheeks of Bano look like red apples."

This would make Bano blush and her cheeks would really turn pink like a fresh rose. She would close her eyes for a moment, feeling shy.

The teacher said, "B for baby."

As Bano heard the word 'baby' she remembered her friend Baby. Her full name was Baby Appy.

Baby Appy lived near her house. They were fast friends. They would do everything together—watching TV, playing, having lunch and dinner and studying.

The day before when Baby Appy returned from her

school, she brought a lollypop. Bano licked it and then offered to Baby Appy as well, saying, "It is very tasty. Taste it at least once."

Baby Appy was busy doing her homework but when Bano offered in a lovely manner, she could not help reach her and taste the lollypop. She said, "How sweet! Just like your cheeks."

"Sh..sh.. Are cheeks sweet? Never," Bano murmured and smiled at Baby Appy.

Baby Appy was everything for Bano. Whatever she would say 'correct' was correct and whatever she would say 'wrong' was wrong. Bano would also sit for studying if Baby Appy would ask her to or to close the T.V. even if it was her favourite programme.

Bano obeyed Baby Appy more than she did to her parents. The credit for Bano's going to school also went to Baby Appy. She did not want to go to school but when Baby Appy persuaded her she got ready. And that too, because it was Baby Appy who dressed her and came with her to school on the first day.

All of a sudden, the teacher's eyes fell on Bano. She asked Bano, "Have you come to school for the first time?" Bano nodded affirmation.

"What is your name?" the teacher asked.

"Bano," came the reply.

"It is your name at home. Tell me the name of the school," asked the teacher.

'Name of the school!' Bano thought. 'Today only papa had told me the name of the school. It is .....yes!.... "Bal Vikas Montessory School" Bano replied.

All the children began to laugh. Teacher also laughed. She said, "Okay! I mean your name that is registered in the school," she tried to clarify. "Baby Appy also called me Bano when she came to school to drop me here," interrupted Bano.

Teacher got irritated. She was unable to

make Bano understand her question. She thought a little and then opened Bano's bag and took out a copy from her bag. In the copy, her name was written as 'Tasneem Bano.'

The teacher said to Bano, "See your name is written on the copy as Tasneem Bano. Remember this is your name in the school."

Then the teacher put the copy back in the bag. Bano said nothing but thought for a while and said, "It is not the name of the school but it is the name of copies and books. You had asked the name of the school but not the name of copies and books. If you had asked the name of copies or books, I would certainly have told you."

Teacher smiled again on Bano's innocent answer. She wanted to kiss her, but it was class. Controlling her feelings she said, "From now onwards I will ask the names of your copies or books. Now study. "B for 'baby', and baby means a child."

Hearing the teacher, Bano again thought, 'Baby means... a child! Baby is the name of my Appy. How it can be possible? Appy is not a child. It should be baby means Appy'.

Teacher asked the students to repeat "B for 'baby' and baby means a child."

Bano thought, 'It appears that teacher does not know that 'baby' means Appy. She desired to point her mistake to the teacher but hesitated and kept quiet.

But Bano continued to think, 'What type of teacher is she? She doesn't seem to know that 'baby' means Appy. Let other students learn 'baby' means a child but I will say 'baby' means Appy, my lovely Appy.

Teacher saw Bano silent and asked her why she was not reciting. Bano mustered her courage and said, "B for baby and 'baby' means Appy".

All the children laughed. The teacher also smiled

and asked her, "How do you know that 'baby' means Appy." Bano replied, "Because the name of my sister is Baby Appy."

The teacher said nothing for a moment. She said after a little while, "It is the name of your sister only. But baby means a child. So you are a baby. All of you are babies!"

But Bano was not ready to surrender so easily. She continued to think, 'Baby Appy is the name given after much consideration by the parents. Hence the teacher must be fooling us. She can not change the truth'.

Then teacher again asked, "Baby means ....?"

"Appy," said Bano slowly.

The teacher again corrected Bano, saying, "Not Appy but child."

But it did not make any difference to Bano. She continued to stick to her point.

The teacher tried to tell her repeatedly but in vain. She got frustrated and scolded her, "You, do what I say otherwise I will punish you. Remember that 'baby' means a child. Bano was scared. The teacher would slap her. She was trembling with fear without saying anything. She had closed her eyes and waited to be slapped by the teacher. But the teacher did not slap Bano. Her anger subsidised with Bano's innocent insistence and she cooled down. She fondled her affectionately. Bano opened her eyes and looked at the teacher hesitantly.

The teacher asked again for almost ten times, "Dear Bano say 'baby' means child." Now the teacher was hopeful that Bano would follow her. Bano looking into the eyes of the teacher said slowly "Appy" and began to weep.

THE CONDITION IS ACCEPTED

The result of half-yearly examination of Anil had spoiled his father's mood. Anil had failed in two subjects. It really mattered much to his father. He was badly upset and bent on punishing his son.

Anil was not at home then.

In anger he went upto Anil's mother and said. "I knew that he would spoil himself by remaining busy all the time in painting. Let him come, I will teach him a lesson."

Mr. Verma, Anil's teacher came to visit them. He sat on the sofa, saying, "You look upset. What happened."

"Please see the result of your student. He has failed in two subjects. In the meantime Anil too happened to come. After greeting his teacher he went to his room."

Mr. Verma said, "I know. It is really a matter of concern. But you are also responsible for this to some extent."

"I am responsible!" exclaimed Anil's father.

"Yes because you failed to understand his feelings properly."

"How can you say so ?" said the father.

"You know that Anil is very interested in painting," said Mr. Verma. "Last year in the painting competition he stood first in the school."

"Yes, I do remember that," said the father and he remembered the day when on returning from his office, he was very happy to know that Anil had got the first prize in painting competition. At the same time he was badly upset to know that Anil had spend a lot of time in its practice. In his eyes the reward in painting was not worth the time wasted for its preparation. He could have given that much time dealing with more important subjects.

Seeing him anxiously silent Mr Verma said further. "You had not appreciated his achievement with the proper advice of handling other subjects as well. With your scolding he became obstinate. This has resulted in his lack of interest in studies. And he began to seek solace in painting which is his hobby."

"But why should he do so?" said the father.

"You say so as you do not know the children's psychology, said Mr. Verma, "They tend to do the things which they are restricted. By adopting such attitude they want to assert their personality."

"Oh! it means ....if ....."

Mr. Verma interrupted , "Yes ! If you had appreciated him instead of scolding, he would have done better in this examination."

"Yes! Last year he stood first in the class," said the father.

Anil came there with the tea for them and put the cups on the table. His father called him and said, "Listen, my dear son. Don't bother for whatever has gone wrong. I too like your paintings and tomorrow I will bring all the material you need for it. But you must show interest in your studies too."

Anil happily nodded his head and promised to study hard to compensate the loss in half yearly exams.

BONDAGE OF LOVE

That day, Jaya was not able to sleep. The lovely face of Tommy appeared before her again and again. Tommy was the name of a dog of her friend, Reena. Tommy was just a puppy but barked very loudly. All over on its white body there were brown spots which looked as if someone had sprinkled the colour carefully on its body.

Jaya liked Tommy very much. She enjoyed playing with Tommy for a long time, making it run after her, holding it in her arms, etc.

Jaya tossed and turned on the bed restlessly. But Tommy remained in her memory. She too wanted to have a cute dog like Tommy to play and also to impress upon her friends. But where could she get such a cute, little dog?

Suddenly, she heard the barking of a puppy outside her house. She got up and went towards the gate of her house. The voice seemed to be coming

from outside.

It was bitter cold and a dense fog also prevailed in the atmosphere. As she opened the gate, she found a little puppy there for its mother but formed no one. She jumped with joy. She looked here and there. There was none. She picked up the puppy and rushed into her room. For Jaya it was as if her dream had come true, that too without any effort.

At first she wiped the puppy with a dry cloth and gave it warm milk. The puppy with its white colour seemed like a ball of cotton. Its round eyes were like big pearls. Jaya looked at it with great affection.

Fondling the puppy, she said, "What is your name? Where is your mother? Why don't you tell me? Oh, you are too little to know all this. But you are so cute. I will keep you with me from today. I will call you Moti. How do you like your name?"

It was 10 p.m. Jaya quickly began to arrange for

Moti to sleep. She took a basket, spread a piece of coarse cloth on it, and put Moti into it to sleep comfortably. Then she covered it with another piece of the cloth. She kept the basket near her bed and lying on her bed kept looking at Moti till she fell asleep.

Next day, Jaya got up early in the morning and got ready for the school. Moti was still sleeping. She fondled on its head and left for school.

That day praising boastfully about Moti was the

only thing that she did with her friends in school.

Even during the class instead of being attentive to her classwork she kept on thinking about Moti, what it must be doing whether it would have eaten or not etc.

Suddenly the teacher saw Jaya and scolded her badly. Jaya felt insulted which she thought was due to Moti. She decided not to talk to Moti anymore.

After the school when she reached home, Moti came to her barking to attract her attention but Jaya didn't notice it. Then it licked her feet and started moving around Jaya but she remained adamant not to react.

All of a sudden, Moti stopped and rushed towards the gate barking loudly.

Though Jaya wanted to take Moti in her arms yet she stood showing her anger. Moti went outside and Jaya stood alone. She remembered the scolding of the teacher. Then she realized that Moti was not at fault for her being scolded. It was her mistake. Now Jaya's heart was filled with love for Moti. She immediately ran towards the gate to catch it.

The scene at the gate was very thrilling. Seeing the gate open, a cow had entered the compound.

But little Moti stood before the cow barking bravely,

not letting the cow to enter the gate. Jaya was very happy to see the bravery of Moti. The cow could crush Moti or throw it aside but it stood like a rock before the cow, barking without pausing.

Jaya picked a stick and drove the cow away. Then she closed the gate. Earlier she had forgotten to close it when she returned home after the school. Now she realised that if the cow was not prevented by Moti from entering the gate, it could have spoiled the plants grown in the lawn.

Then she turned to Moti who was looking up at her with appealing eyes to be noticed.

Jaya could not keep herself from picking up Moti in her arms. Caressing affectionately on its body, she also realised her mistake for unnecessarily getting annoyed with Moti.

DREAM OF SUMMI

The moment Pooja entered the room, she saw Summi sitting near the cot facing the wall. She had her back towards the door. Pooja reached behind Summi tip toeing not letting the latter feel about her movement. She knew the sound of her footsteps could distract her. She saw Summi with a book in her hands.

The first page of the book of Hindi alphabets which started with the first letter of *anar* (pomegranate). There was the picture of pomegranate which appeared attractive. Summi was learning her lesson. Soon she began to think about the taste of pomegranate which she knew to be very tasty. She decided to ask her papa to bring some for her.

Summi then turned over to the second page. A Hindi letter with the picture of a ripe yellow mango.

Actually the word *aam* (mango) starts with that letter.

The very sight of juicy, sweet mango made her mouth water. Her cheeks turned reddish, eyes began to shine and licking her rose-petal-like lips, she said, "This is the ripe mango! The king of fruits! It is very sweet!"

She took a pause and continued. "My *didi* also looks like a princess when she goes to school in her uniform. But mummy does not let me go to school. I will also appear as princess wearing red skirt, white shoes, white socks, black tie, and red ribbon. All will love me ....."

Pooja was listening to Summi standing like a statue behind her and was enjoying her talking. Summi continued, "I will go to school and will study. I will also win prizes like *didi*. Then mummy will pick me up in her arms and kiss me......."

There was a glow of happiness on her face. She had reached school in her imagination. Pooja slowly put her bag on the table and stealthily went out of the room. Summi was quite unaware of Pooja's entering and leaving the room. She was visualising the size of her class- room, saying, "It would be bigger than this room."

Then she stretched her hands like wings of butterfly saying, "This much! There will be many children in the school like my dolls. I will go to school daily. I will sit on the front row as my *didi* says that good children always sit in the front. But if there would be no seat for me in the front row then? No, I will sit only on the front row. I am also good in studies. I know the counting up to twenty, ...one ......two ......three...... eighteen and then!"

She forgot and after a while said, "Anyway I will learn again. Even mummy once forgot to bring the chocolate for me. I will study hard and obey my

teacher. But what my teacher will be like? Perhaps like my mummy. No! She will be wearing specs and have a cane in her hand! But I am a good girl, so why should I fear? But papa scolded me yesterday calling me mischievous. But I will not do anything wrong in the school. I will always obey the teacher. Then she will love me and make me the monitor of the class. And I will control the class in her absence. I will keep the children under control. The teacher will punish the bad students. *Didi* says that the teacher asks them to become cock in the class. I will manage the class. But how the teacher makes them cock? Does he have a magic wand? Then it would be a fun to be a cock! Other children must be teasing those who become cock. But why would one commit mischief to be punished to become a cock?"

She continued, "...Cock is not a good animal as it

always roams about in the garbage. I do not like it. I am a good girl. Why should I be a cock? I will study hard. I will write to fill a copy daily and will ask mummy for a new copy everyday."

Suddenly, Summy stopped to speak. She saw mummy standing in front of her and she had a new copy in her hand.

Mummy said, " Summy, take your new copy."

"For me!" Summy exclaimed. She could not believe her eyes.

"Yes, for you. You have grown up. Now practice on this new copy. Next week you will be admitted in the school." Summi was very happy. She quickly hugged her mother. She knew that her dream of going to school is about to be real.

GOLDEN OPPORTUNITY

Intermediate examinations were to be started from that day. The examination commenced from the first date of the month with practical of chemistry. All the students reached the college with full preparations and were eager to appear in the test. They assembled at the lawn in front of the chemistry laboratory. Suddenly, bell rang and all the students made a queue near the lab. I saw my watch. It was 9.35 a.m. and the test was to start at 10.00 a.m. The students were supposed to be on their places, 15 minutes before the test. So I also stood in the line.

The teacher noted down the names of the students serially and asked them to deposit their practical files with him and began to send them to laboratory.

On my turn I deposited the file and wrote down my name in the register. I was given two matters to be

recognized. Smelling them I entered the lab.

I was impressed with the atmosphere of the lab that day. Things were arranged in proper order unlike the other days. Acids and chemicals were in full stock.

To our surprise there was a supply of water in the taps and the burners were filled with gas. Moreover, the roll numbers were also written on the desks.

I saw my file. My roll number was 30. So I occupied the seat bearing the number 30. After some time the lab assistant gave two types of powder with a test tube to each and every student. I took out the things from the bag and started the experiment.

This batch consisted of only 35 students. They were to be interviewed along with their practical tests. The examiner Singh Sir was known for his punctuality. He did not waste time for viva. He reached a student in front of my seat and asked questions orally.

The questions put up by Singh Sir were related to the practical being done by each student. He listened to the answers with great patience. Then he put his remark on the copy and moved ahead.

I concentrated on my practical. Luckily the practical test given to me was very easy. I complete my work soon. Thereafter, I turned my attention to Singh Sir again. I tried my best to understand the nature of the questions being put up by him.

All of a sudden, Narottam Sir, the chemistry teacher of the college entered the lab. Singh Sir was checking the copy of Satish. Narottam Sir said to Singh Sir, "This boy is a very promising student of the college. Please take care of him." Singh Sir looked at Satish and assured him, "I shall consider about it."

Satish was standing in front of my seat. So, I was curiously looking at him. Singh Sir picked his practical copy and said, "Your performance seems to be

good. Well, tell me from which chapter I should ask you question."

"Sir, compound," said Satish.

"But it is a very lengthy chapter. Will you be able to answer the questions?" asked Singh Sir.

"Yes sir, I am ready," said Satish.

Singh Sir asked him total ten questions one by one. Satish answered seven of them correctly.

Then Singh Sir asked him, "How many marks should I give to you."

The practical test carried thirty marks. Satish, seeing the suitable opportunity, requested for full marks.

But Singh Sir said, "You do not deserve full marks but if you promise to labour hard in future ....."

"Sure, I will do my best. I assure you, sir," Satish said.

Hearing Satish, Singh Sir took his copy of practical test and wrote 30 in the space provided for the marks on the front page. Then he smiled and went ahead to the other students.

Seeing all this, the palpitation of my heart increased considerably. My self-confidence boosted, provoking me not to lose this opportunity at any cost.

But there was none to recommend me as Narottam Sir did to Satish.

"Should I try myself," I thought. "I have to do something to avail this opportunity."

But next moment I thought over it again and asked myself, "Is it right? The teacher may take it for my impudence."

Thinking deeply, I decided not to lose this opportunity. I was determined to test my confidence. It would be a folly to lose this opportunity.

After some time Singh Sir came to me but then the bell rang. There were six students left for the test. Singh Sir wanted to finish the viva of all the students so he called all of us to him.

This made me lose all my hope for the full marks. I felt as if someone had snatched the precious gift of thirty marks from my hand. If I failed to do something, I shall be left repenting.

As such I got firmly resolved and told Singh Sir "Sir, you may ask any question from the chapter of radioactivity." At this Singh Sir was surprised and looked at me. I looked resolved having self-confidence. Perhaps he did not believe me.

"But if any of your answers is wrong, then?" he tried to intimidate me.

"You can do whatever you like," I replied slowly. "I will resort to minus marking if any of the answer

happened to be wrong," said Singh Sir.

As I was ready for all challenges, I agreed. Singh Sir also asked other students, "Do you all agree with this condition?"

But other students were not ready to take this risk, so they refused.

Singh sir looked at me and began to ask questions related to the chapter of my choice. He asked twelve questions which I answered confidently. All the answers were correct. Singh sir became very happy and said, "You deserve full marks I don't see any reason to cut even one mark".

Then, with a smile on his face Singh Sir patted my back, took my practical copy and wrote 30/30 marks on it and signed it.

My joy knew no bound with this achievement which was not only for obtaining hundred present marks in the practical test but also for believing in myself.

AJAY TURNED TEACHER

The students were busy talking, playing and making a noise in their classroom. The teacher was not present in the class. All of a sudden someone opened the door and the mischief making of the students came to a pause.

It was the monitor of the class, Ajay with a stick in his hand. He was also having a specs on his eyes. He entered the classroom and looking at the boys said, "Hello students! Today, the teacher is on leave. So I will teach you. Are you ready?"

All the boys said, "Yes sir!" Ajay became very happy. He sat on the chair saying, "I will test your general knowledge today."

"Yes sir!" Echoed the voice in the classroom. Ajay bore a serious look on his face and asked, "Anwar, tell the name of a *kali* (bud) which never turns into flower throughout its life."

"Sir," *chhipkali* (lizard)."

"Oh!, The boys of this class are very smart!" murmured Ajay.

Then he adjusted the specs and asked, "Prasoon, can you tell whether the earth is round or flat?"

Prasoon stood up and said, "Sir if I climb on a very tall tree, then I can tell, how the earth looks."

"Now Akhilesh, tell me whether tea is useful or harmful," said Ajay.

He replied, "It is useful if it is served free of cost and harmful if we pay for it."

Everybody laughed and Ajay got them silent.

Then Ajay asked Sumit, "Do you know why the stars are not visible during the day?"

Sumit told innocently, "But, sir,

we can see the stars during the day as well. Sir once my elder brother slapped me hard and made me see the stars during the day."

Hearing the reply the whole class laughed. Suddenly, a voice came from behind, "Sumit do you remember, how many stars were there? Didn't you count them?" And then again laughter echoed in the class.

Ajay also laughed but soon he controlled himself. He asked Firoz, "Suppose an automatic robot comes to beat your brother then what will you say?"

"Sir, the gift of science," said Firoz promptly. All the students laughed again. Even Ajay couldn't help laughing.

Ajay wanted to get the class to be serious. He sat on the chair silently and asked, "David, tell the name of the grandson of Akbar's grandfather." But David did not speak. Ajay asked another question, "Who invented the sweet *Jalebi?*" David still remained silent.

Seeing David silent Ajay got upset. Moving his stick in the air to frighten David, he said, "You know nothing about history, geography and science. After all what do you know?"

He said, "Sir I know you." His answer made all the students laugh.

Ajay got upset. He was serious so he scolded them, "Keep silence otherwise the fly will hit your teeth."

The students chuckled a bit but to see their Ajay, the teacher upset they kept shut. Then he asked Kishore, "What are the uses of ears?"

Kishore said, "Sir, you twist our ears and also make us hold our ears when we are punished."

The students laughed again. But Ajay warned them saying, "Stop laughing boys! otherwise I will use your ears." Then, looking at Raja he said, "Tell, why do the people having beard touch their beard again and again?"

"They must be counting the hair on their bread!" saying so Raja laughed and so did the whole cross. The teacher got angry and he said to him, "Keep your hands up for whole period."

"But I cannot keep my hands up," Raja cut a sorry figure.

"Why? What is the problem in doing that?" asked the teacher.

"Because if I do that, my half pants will slip down my waist," said Raja innocently. But the whole class burst into laughter.

Teacher too smiled at his genuine problem and said, "All right. Sit down." Then he asked Sukhvinder, "Suppose you purchased some books for Rs. 50.00, a pen for Rs. 10.00 and two copies for Rs. 25,00, how much money will you pay the shopkeeper."

Sukhvinder thought a little and said, "Sir two rupees!"

The teacher (Ajay) got badly upset and said, "How can you pay two rupees for so many things?"

"Because I have only two rupees," said Sukhvinder, showing a two rupees note.

Now the teacher wanted to get the class over. So he said, "From tomorrow the school will be closed for ten days. Then your examination will begin, okay! Does anybody want to ask anything?"

Udaya at once raised his hand and asked, "Tell us, in which press our question papers will be printed?"

"Well, come here, you shall be punished." But then the door was opened by a teacher. Seeing him, Ajay tried to slip out but the teacher caught him by his ears. The whole class laughed. The teacher twisted his ears which pained so much that he got up. "Oh it was a dream!" he said and began to recollect the whole incident. A smile appeared on his face. He again lay down on the bed hoping for another good dream.

WHO IS AT FAULT

Once there lived a woodcutter named Nankoo. One day, he was sharpening the edge of his axe on a stone slab. A snail was there who got disturbed by its sound. So, he bit the woodcutter on his foot and slipped into the bushes.

Nankoo writhed with pain and in a fit of rage and hit the coconut tree with full might with his axe. The coconut tree got hurt, so in turn he dropped a big coconut on the ground. There was a cock nearby, picking up grains and it was hit hard by the coconut. He ran for his life.

There was an anthill, which the cock destroyed in anger. The ants ran here and there in panic. Meanwhile, a black snake happened to pass by. The angry ants got all over his body. Being helpless to do anything the snake ran for his life.

But the snake was much

enraged. He saw a pig coming towards him. The angry snake cooled his anger by biting the pig. The pig became mad due to painful poisonous snakebite. So he uprooted the nearby bushes. There was a bat hanging from a branch of the bushes. He flew in panic and entered the ear of an elephant.

The elephant became restless and began to run here and there. Being badly enraged the elephant uprooted a rock. The rock rolled down and fell on a the hut of an old woman. The hut was damaged badly.

The old woman got furious to see her hut damaged and cried, "Oh you, bloody rock! You have destroyed my hut. Now pay for the loss immediately."

The rock was badly confused and frustrated to hear for paying for damaging the hut. How could she pay for the losses. She apologised to the old woman and said, "I am not at fault. It was the elephant who is responsible for your loss. Had he not hit me, I would not have tumbled down to you. So you should ask the elephant for damage of your hut."

The old woman agreed and went to the elephant and said, "O elephant! My hut has been destroyed due to the rock that you had up rooted. So you pay for the loss."

The elephant was astonished to see the old woman asking for compensation. He said to her, "I am not at fault. The wicked bat had entered in my ear, so I ran here and there in a panic and the rock was uprooted. Therefore please ask the bat for the compensation."

The elephant seemed to be right. So the old woman rushed to the bat. The bat was trying to sleep, with

his eyes closed. The old woman's asking for the loss made him angry. He said, "Why should I pay for the loss. Go to the pig who uprooted the bushes compelling me run in a haste to a safer place."

Saying so the bat closed his eyes. The old woman wished to teach a lesson to the bat but acting wisely she went in search of the pig who was rolling on the mud. She asked the pig for the compensation for damaging his hut. The pig was enraged to hear her and said, "It is all due to the snake that bit me. So go and ask him to pay for the damage."

Thus, the old woman got much irritated. But what else could she do? Then she went in search of the snake and found him near his hole. He was moaning due to pain caused by the ants. He said, "I was going to the garden when the ants attacked me for no fault of mine." With these words the snake started sobbing. Seeing the tears in the eyes of the snake, the old woman was moved herself. She went from there in search of the ants.

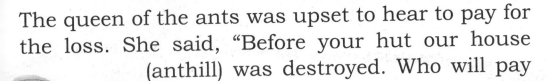

The queen of the ants was upset to hear to pay for the loss. She said, "Before your hut our house (anthill) was destroyed. Who will pay for our loss? You should go to the cock who attacked us and destroyed our home."

So far the old woman was badly exhausted but she was determined to receive the compensation. Therefore, she proceeded further in search of the cock.

The old woman found the cock moaning due to the pain on his back. He told her that it was caused by a coconut. He advised her to go to the coconut tree.

Following the advice of the cock, the old woman, though in frustration, reached the coconut tree. She asked the tree for compensating the loss of her hut. Then he said,

"It was not my fault to drop a coconut. Why did the woodcutter hit me? You must ask the woodcutter for the compensation."

By now the old woman was utterly frustrated, but she reached the woodcutter Nankoo who was applying medicine on his foot where the snail had bitten. When she asked him to pay for her damaged hut, he said, "You can see how badly the snail bit me. So, he is responsible for your loss. Go and ask him for it."

Thereafter, she went to the snail who was sitting at the pond. She abused him a lot and asked for the compensation. The snail heard the old woman without blaming others for his fault.

He felt so ashamed of himself for being the cause of damaging her hut that he hid himself in a shell and did not come out. The old woman waited for long for the snail to came out, but in vain. Till today, the snail has not come out of its shell.

HIMEE'S SACRIFICE

There was an innocent fairy whose name was Himee. Himee was living with her parents in the mountainous regions of Fairyland. The family's responsibility was to cause snowfall on the earth Her parents and Himee looked as white as snow. She looked like a white doll but whenever she laughed her cheeks would turn reddish. She liked the greenery, Himalayas, the kids etc. on our earth. Whenever she heard about the people of earth she would be curious to go there. She wanted to enjoy the company of the children to run with them and play games with them.

One day she said to her mother, "Mummy, I want to go to the earth to enjoy its beauty."

Her mother smiled at her and said, "But my dear as per the rules of Fairyland one is not allowed to go to the earth before the age of twenty years."

" Why is it so?" asked Himee.

The mother replied, "Because all are bound by this rule and if anyone violates this rule then he or she is not allowed to return to Fairyland." Her mother's answer disappointed Himee. She thought again, 'On attaining the age of twenty I will defiantly go to the earth.' But when she calculated her age she found it was only twelve and she would have to wait eight more years. She was too curious to wait for such a long time. Therefore, she kept on thinking to find a solution of this problem.

One day, sitting on a huge rock she was enjoying the beauty of the earth. The ice was falling on earth from ice ocean. It appeared as if several white fairies with their open wings were going to the earth. All of a sudden an idea struck her mind, "Why not to change myself into a piece of ice and so no one would be able to recognize me. She immediately, changed herself into ice, mixed with the ice ocean and reached the earth. Now, Himee looked like a ball of ice.

Himee was very happy on reaching the earth. She found herself in midst of the ice. Even the plants and trees were covered with ice. She wanted to play with the children but due to the snowfall they were inside the houses. So Himee flew towards the fields.

Himee kept on flying in the sky for a long time and got down in the fields. As she was very tired, she sat under tree and began to rest. But the tree became very cold because of her. He requested her to go to some other place otherwise it would fall ill.

Himee was stunned to hear the tree. She flew further and saw a school ground where children were playing. Himee sat on a stone and began to watch the children.

All of a sudden, Himee saw a boy who looked sad. Perhaps, he was not allowed to play with the other boys.

Himee flew to the boy and sat on his head. The head

of the boy became cold due to the ice fairy, Himee. The boy became very happy.

After some time the bell rang to let the school get over. All the boys ran to their houses. That boy also happily ran to his home. But by the time, he reached home he had high fever. His mother took him to the doctor. Seeing the boy in fever, Himee became very sad. She flew from there.

Then she saw a calf playing with other calves. She wished to play with the calf. She flew and sat on the head of the calf. The touch of Himee, the ice fairy made the calf happy. He ran to his mother cow. But when she saw Himee sitting on the head of the calf, she got angry and said, "Run away from here. Do not make my son ill."

Himee became very sad to hear the cow. She thought, 'I came here to meet these people but they think of me as an enemy.' She lost all her interest on

earth. She thought, 'People should not interfere with the rules of the nature. How can ice survive in hot place?'

Himee laughed on her own folly. She flew back towards Fairyland. But while still on the way she heard a voice, "You have violated the rule of Fairyland, so you cannot come to Fairyland."

Himee was disappointed to hear the voice. A wave of sadness appeared on her face. What could she do now? She wandered aimlessly for some time. Then she saw a bird, dying of thirst. She thought, "I have to wander aimlessly for whole life, so it would be better to save the life of this bird."

Thinking this. Himee entered the beak of the bird and turned into water. The bird drank the water and his life was saved. He thanked Himee and flew to his home. Since then whenever people talk about the greatness of others, that bird recollects the sacrifice of Himee. He takes a great pride on the ice fairy Himee who sacrificed her own life to save his life.

THE NEST

There was a very beautiful tree in the forest of Sundervan. The tree was as tall as a palm tree. One would have to stretch his/her neck back to have a look at it. It was so huge and expanded around its trunk that it could accommodate a small village under it. The unlimited number of branches with leaves on them didn't let the sunrays reach the ground below it.

This tree was the oldest of all the trees of the forest. So all the birds and animals paid respect to it. Every year during the spring season the new leaves growing on it would give it a look of wearing new cloth. But with the setting in of autumn, the dry straws and leaves would pile under it. The animals

would hop, jump and crush them under their feet. This made the straws very sad.

One day a pair of pigeons came there. They were very happy to see such a tree which they had never seen before. So one of the pigeons said to the other, "How nice the place is! There is no shortage of dearth of straws as well. Why should we not make our nest here?"

The other pigeon agreed to the proposal, "Yes, why not? This is the best place for us to make our nest."

Both the pigeons took a round of the tree. Then they selected a big branch for making the nest. There were several small branches around the main branch giving it a bowl-like look. The straws could be arranged very easily there.

Both the pigeons began to make their nest. They picked up the straws from the piles below the tree, then they arranged them to build the nest.

The straw picked up by the pigeons thought themselves lucky and felt happy as they were being placed on a height of the tree. While they had been

crushed under the feet of those who passed by the tree. Now they would no longer have to be crushed like that.

The pigeons kept working tirelessly without a pause till their nest was built. It looked very beautiful. The pigeons were very happy to have got a suitable place to live. They would wander about during the day and in the evening would come back to take rest. They would keep talking with each other and then sleep comfortably.

The straws also were as happy as the pigeons because they were not being crushed any longer. Now they could enjoy the fresh air in the height.

Now during the course of time, the straws began to feel bored. They were fed up with the life of the nest, where they had to bear the stink of the pigeons excreta.

Gradually the thinking of the straws changed. They forgot the old days when they used to be crushed by the passers-by. Now they were living on the height of the tree, but were not feeling well. When the pigeons went away for picking up the grains the straws would make fun of them. One day the pigeons came to know about his. They felt sad with their attitude. One of the pigeons tried to persuade them, "My dear straws, you should not be so egoistic because ego always leads to disaster."

A straw murmured, "Don't forget that you live in the nest made up by us. Keep your preaching to yourself."

Pigeons did not like the way the straws talked. One of them said, "But the nest was made by us."

"So what? It is made up of us. If we were not there, you would not be able to make the nest," said one of the straws with pride.

Now they realised that the straws have become unreasonable. One of the pigeons said furiously, "Did all of you forget how useless you were, scattered on the earth, before being picked up by us for this nest? Don't forget, had we not picked you up to make the nest, you would have got trampled and destroyed."

"So what? You are living here at our mercy otherwise, you would be homeless," said a straw.

The pigeons kept their cool despite being provoked by the straws. But the straws took it otherwise. They thought that the pigeons were afraid of them. So they said, "We have tolerated you for long. Now go somewhere else other wise..."

"Other wise what?" the pigeons said.

"We will throw you down," said the straws.

Pigeons lost their cool to hear them. They decided to teach them a lesson. They destroyed the nest within no time and threw it down. Both the pigeons flew in search of another place. The nest fell and got scattered on the filthy ground. The straws were crushed by the animals. Thus, their ego brought them back to where they had been. They had nothing to gain now by repenting.

MOTHER'S ADVICE

There was an earthworm. He was very mischievous. His name was Chikee. He was living with his mother under the ground in a hole near the river. Having no work to do, he used to roam here and there and keep himself busy in mischievous activities teasing others. So far as eating food was concerned he had nothing but soil to eat.

Chikee was fed up with his monotonous existence doing nothing more than roaming in the dark and eating earth.

The mother of Chikee used to tell him about another world, the earth with mountains, rivers, houses and the people living there.

So, Chikee often imagined about that world on the earth and would get thrilled.

One day while thinking about the world above, Chikee happened to hear the strange sound above his head. Her mother at once came there and asked him, " Hurry up! Come down with me otherwise we are going to be caught," he followed his mother down, asking what the matter was. After some time

they reached too deep to be harmed by the digger.

Now, his mother said, "Someone was digging the earth. The people living above us dig the earth to catch us and use us as food for alluring the fish to be caught."

Chikee was scared to hear all that and hid behind his mother, saying, "These people are very bad."

Some days passed but Chikee had not forgotten the interesting world on the earth. Despite frequent warning of his mother, he insisted on going up and take a walk there.

One day Chikee adamantly asked his mother to go up. She said, "Don't even think about going up otherwise birds will eat you. They are very dangerous."

"All right! I will never ask you to go there," said Chikee looking horrified.

But after some days the attraction and thrilling overcame his fear. He, without letting his mother know, had been waiting for an opportunity to slip out in the world above. He thought, "I am not afraid of the birds, I will teach them a lesson if they attack me."

Thus, Chikee would often lie in wait for a suitable opportunity but he never had any.

One day his mother was feeling unwell. While resting she fell asleep. He did not want to lose this most awaited chance and slipped out on the surface.

It was evening. The cold wind was blowing. Chikee was very happy to be there. Moreover, he did not see any such danger as his mother had warned against.

He crept towards the river hearing rhythmical flow of water. He saw some frogs, so lively and hopping around here and there. He was very happy to leave that dark world under the earth.

He saw a tree in front of him. Its branches were waving in the air. Chikee wished to swing in the air. But he recollected the warning of his mother about

the birds living on the tree. So he stopped and left the idea of enjoying swinging and walked away from the tree.

Then, he saw some houses at some distance and began to count them. But failed in doing so.

He kept moving further. His eyes fell on a beautiful flower on a small tree. He touched the flower and felt ticked. He laughed at the foolish advice of his mother against visiting such a wonderful place.

Then a kite happened to fly over there and saw Chikee. He swooped, caught it and flew away.

The kite had caught Chikee in his beak. Feeling too much pain, Chikee thought that the bird would soon eat him. He was scared. Now Chikee remembered the advice of his mother, against going up in the world. He was repenting now. His life was in danger. But then he thought that only just repenting would not do. Instead he needed to do

something to save his life.

Then only he remembered the tickling he had felt on touching the little flower. An idea struck his mind. He wrapped himself around the neck of the bird and began to wriggle his body. This produced tickling round the neck of the bird.

Feeling the tickle around his neck, the bird was unable to hold its grip on Chikee, opened his mouth and loosened, he at once jumped out on to the earth. Fortunately he fell near his hole.

The kite was too frustrated for losing his prey. But before he would reach Chikee again, the latter entered his hole. Now he took a sigh of relief. Though his body was wounded being caught in the beak, he was happy to be alive. He now rushed to his mother thinking that mother was really right.

THE GREAT GRAND TREE

Sukkhu was tired by digging the foundation of his house. So he sat on the cot to take rest for a while. He wiped out his sweat with a towel and drank water.

This year Sukkhu had a good crop. He wanted to build a nice house by selling the crop. Therefore, he was digging the foundation.

Sukkhu was living with his wife and a son, though his house was good, yet during the rainy season water oozed into the house through the roof causing much trouble. So, he had decided to build a pucca house.

There was a *neem* tree at the plot the house was to be constructed. This tree was planted by the grandfather of Sukkhu when he was a child. During all those years, it had become a big tree. With the perching of the birds of different colours on the tree, a lively atmosphere was created in the evening. Its cool shade was very soothing during the scorching summer's days.

"Father, I have brought the axe," Sukkhu heard his son's voice.

"Keep it there," said Sukhu. "Let me rest for a while then I will begin to cut the tree."

The boy put the axe near the tree and went off to play.

Meanwhile with the cool breeze under the tree relieved tired Sukkhu and

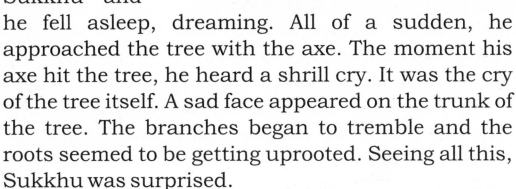

he fell asleep, dreaming. All of a sudden, he approached the tree with the axe. The moment his axe hit the tree, he heard a shrill cry. It was the cry of the tree itself. A sad face appeared on the trunk of the tree. The branches began to tremble and the roots seemed to be getting uprooted. Seeing all this, Sukkhu was surprised.

But before he could say anything he heard a voice, "Do you know, what you are going to do."

Sukkhu was now more surprised as the voice seemed to be familiar to him. He looked around but none was to be seen.

"Reply my question," Sukku heard the voice again and this time he could recognise the voice. It was his grandfather's voice. "I am going to cut this tree," Sukkhu spoke in bewilderment. "Here I will build my house."

His grand father spoke in a sad voice, "I am sad that you failed to understand the importance of this tree. Listen, I, your grand father, had planted this tree and nourished it like a son. Hundreds of birds take shelter here. During the summer its shade cools not only you but also it relieves the fatigue of several passers-by." Sukkhu was spellbounded hearing his grand father. The voice continued, "It provides you wood for making food. Its green stick is used to clean the teeth. Moreover the oil of its fruits, the bark and the leaves are used for curing the diseases. But you are bent upon cutting it for your selfishness. Is it not a sin you are going to commit?" The question shattered Sukkhu badly. He was awoke now. His dream was broken. He was very sad with tears rolling down his eyes. Suddenly, he got up and hugged the tree round its trunk saying, "I am sorry, Pardon me Baba."

The tears rolling down his eyes fell on the roots of the tree. The heavy wind were bowing the branches. It appeared as if the tree, like his grandfather wished to pick up Sukkhu in his lap. Sukkhu, from that day, began to call the tree as "Baba Tree."